Modern Curriculum Press
BEGINNING
TO
READ
Series

The
Magic
Beans

ISBN: 0-8136-5553-6
Printed in the United States of America

17 18 19 20   06 05 04

Modern
Curriculum
Press

Pearson Learning Group

1-800-321-3106
www.pearsonlearning.com

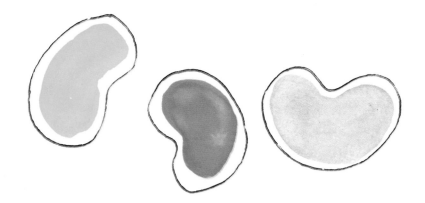

The
Magic
Beans

Margaret Hillert

Illustrated by Mel Pekarsky

Oh, look.

Here is something funny.

One is red.

One is blue.

One is yellow.

One little one.

Two little ones.

Three little ones.

Look, look, look.

Go down here.

Go down in here, little ones.

Oh, oh.

Look and see.

Here is something little.

Up it comes.

Oh, my. Oh, my.

It is big, big, big.

I can go up.

See me go up.

Up, up, up and away.

Look here, look here.

I see a house.

It is a big, big house.

I want to go in.

In I go.

Jump, jump, jump.

It is big in here.

It is big for little me.

Here is something.

It is not big.

It is little and red.

Look, look.

It can work.

It can make something.

Come to me.

Come to me.

I want you.

Come to my house.

Away we go.

Oh, look here.

Here is something for Mother.

Something for my mother.

And here is something.

We can play it.

We can make it play.

It is fun to play.

Come, come.

Come to my house.

Come to my mother.

Here we go.

Away, away, away.

Oh, my.

Here comes something.

Something big.

Where can I go?

Help, help.

Here I go.

Run, run, run.

And here I go.

Down, down, down.

Mother, Mother.

Here I come.

Help me. Help me.

We can work.

We can make it come down.

Here, Mother.

Here is something for you.

Margaret Hillert, author of several books in the MCP Beginning-To-Read Series, is a writer, poet, and teacher.

The Magic Beans

Delightful illustrations accompany this favorite tale of Jack and the Beanstalk which is told in 44 preprimer words.

Word List

7 oh	in	to
look	**10** and	jump
here	see	**15** for
is	up	**16** not
something	it	**17** work
funny	comes	make
one	**11** my	**18** you
red	big	we
blue	**12** I	**19** mother
yellow	can	**20** play
8 little	me	fun
two	away	**23** where
three	**13** a	**24** help
9 go	house	run
down	**14** want	